This Book Belongs To

_____

_____

_____

Welcome to the
Wild Animal Adventure!

Hello, Young Artist!

In this book, you will meet 50 wild animals and learn interesting information about them.

They are waiting for you and want you to decorate their world.

You can do it yourself, with friends or parents.

I am sure you will be interested in watching how animals are transformed and come to life after you decorate them with different colors.

Have a nice trip to the world of wild animals!

Test color page

Giraffe

Giraffes sleep only about 20 minutes to 2 hours per day!

Elephant

Elephants can "hear" with their feet by sensing ground vibrations.

Lion

A lion's roar can be heard up to 5 miles away.

Zebra

No two zebras have the same stripe pattern, just like human fingerprints.

Kangaroo

Kangaroos can't walk backward
due to their large tails.

Penguin

Penguins propose to their mates with a pebble.

6

Sloth

Sloths can take up to a month to digest a single meal.

Hippo

Hippos can run faster than humans on land, reaching speeds of 30 mph.

Panda

Pandas spend up to 14 hours a day eating bamboo.

Raccoon

Raccoons can open nearly any container or lock, thanks to their nimble paws.

Ostrich

Ostriches have the largest eyes of any land animal, even larger than their brains.

Cheetah

Cheetahs can accelerate from 0 to 60 mph in just a few seconds.

Koala

Koalas sleep up to 20 hours a day, mainly due to their low-energy diet of eucalyptus leaves.

Monkey

Some monkeys can understand and use money in experiments.

Camel

The camel lives in the hot desert, can live for a long time without water and likes to spit.

Hyena

Hyenas have a laugh-like call, which is used to communicate their social status.

16

Wombat

Wombats produce cube-shaped poop to mark their territory.

Porcupine

Porcupines have around 30,000 quills, which they replace regularly.

Armadillo

Armadillos can hold their breath for up to 6 minutes.

Meerkat

Meerkats have a designated "sentry" to watch for predators while the others forage.

Flamingo

Flamingos are naturally white; they get their pink color from their diet.

Rhino

A rhino's horn is made of keratin, the same substance as human nails and hair.

Crocodile

Crocodiles can't stick their tongues out.

Baboon

Baboons have dog-like muzzles, but they are more closely related to humans and apes.

Moose

A moose's antlers can spread up to 6 feet across.

Alligator

Alligators can live up to 100 years in captivity.

Anteater

Anteaters have tongues that can reach up to 2 feet in length.

Beaver

Beavers' teeth never stop growing, which helps them gnaw on wood continuously.

Polar Bear

Polar bears have black skin under their white fur, which helps absorb heat.

Lemur

Lemurs can recognize members of their group by their unique scent.

Opossum

Lemurs can recognize members of their group by their unique scent.

31

Bison

Bison can reach speeds of up to 35 mph despite their large size.

Ibex

Ibexes are incredible climbers, often scaling near-vertical cliffs.

Lynx

Lynxes have large, padded paws that act like natural snowshoes.

Narwhal

Narwhals are known as "unicorns of the sea" due to their long,

Gazelle

Gazelles can leap up to 10 feet in the air to evade predators.

Okapi

Okapis are the only living relative of giraffes.

Jaguar

Jaguars have the strongest bite of any big cat, capable of crushing turtle shells.

Aardvark

Aardvarks can dig a hole faster than a group of six men using shovels.

Walrus

Walruses use their long tusks to pull themselves out of the water onto ice.

Emu

Emus can sprint up to 30 mph and can swim, too.

Caracal

Caracals can leap up to 10 feet into the air to catch birds in flight.

42

Mongoose

Mongooses are highly resistant to snake venom, especially cobra venom.

Tapir

Tapirs have excellent swimming abilities and can use their snouts as snorkels.

Wolverine

Wolverines can travel up to 15 miles in a day while hunting.

Manatee

Manatees can swim up to 20 miles per day searching for food.

Quokka

Quokkas are known as "the world's happiest animal" because of their smiling faces.

Dugong

Dugongs are closely related to elephants, not other marine mammals.

Komodo Dragon

The Komodo Dragon is the largest lizard in the world, its length reaches 13 feet and weight up to 300 pounds.

49

Alpaca

Alpacas hum when they are curious, content, or concerned.

Made in the USA
Monee, IL
18 November 2024

70493536R00057